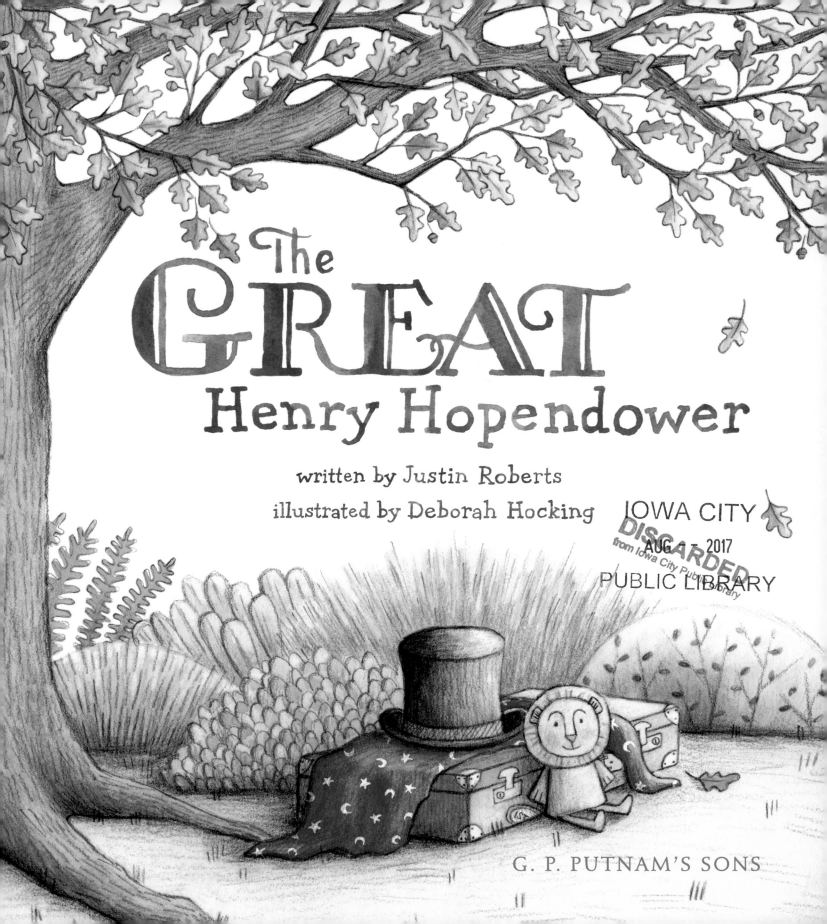

The GREAT
Henry Hopendower

written by Justin Roberts

illustrated by Deborah Hocking

G. P. PUTNAM'S SONS

Henry awoke. The sun scratched the freshly polished floors. Henry's hair, darting in every conceivable direction, seemed to float in midair.

He raised his finger and announced suddenly, and to no one in particular, "I'm off to find magic!"

Henry ducked into his closet,
then reappeared holding a bright
red checkered suit.

Henry remembered the
day his grandpa had given
him the suit.

"Henry, to be a magician, you have to notice that magic is everywhere."

His grandpa held a small silver coin in his hand, closed his fist and chanted the magic words:

"Blah bloppolis, flooey floppilus, tohu, bohu, lickety-split!"

When Grandpa opened his hand, the coin was gone.

Still lost in thought, Henry got dressed and put all of his magical things into a brown leather suitcase. He snapped it shut and proclaimed, "I'm the Great Henry Hopendower!"

He bowed.
To no applause.

Henry walked confidently through the kitchen. "Mom, I'm off to find magic!"

Henry had loved
magic for as long as
he could remember.

Whenever he would visit his grandpa's house,
Henry felt magic all around him: the creak of the
floors that would sing with Henry's every step and
the wobbly cuckoo clock with the small wooden
bird that would appear and then vanish.

And of course, Grandpa's famous leaning tower of pancakes, which tipped but never toppled.

Magic, Henry thought.

But most magical of all was Grandpa himself.

"My magician.

Where have you been?

I thought you had disappeared."

One time, Henry asked,
"Grandpa, what is magic?"
"Magic? Why, it's
something from nothing.
And it's all around us," his
grandpa said, pointing to
their reflections in the mirror.

Grandpa splashed some magic-scented water on his stubbly cheeks. "And, Henry, when we notice there is magic, truly impossible things can happen."

Grandpa reached behind Henry's ear and pulled out a bright, shiny coin.

Alone in his yard, Henry carefully opened the suitcase

"I'm the Great Henry Hopendower. I'm here to do truly impossible things."

Henry took off his hat and showed the audience that it was empty.

and assembled
his audience.

Henry smiled.
He felt like a magician.

"I'm going to
pull a white rabbit
out of this hat."

Henry reached
inside the hat and
felt . . .

Nothing.

He quickly tried
Grandpa's magic words:

"Blah bloppolis,
flooey floppilus,
tohu, bohu,
lickety-split!"

He reached in again.
Still nothing.

Henry thought of the day not long ago when he
and his mother had stood in Grandpa's empty house.
Everything was gone, but Henry could still smell
Grandpa's magic-scented water hanging in the air.
"Henry," his mother had said, "this brown leather
suitcase would be perfect for all of your magic things."

Now, with his hand in the empty hat,
Henry remembered what Grandpa had said.
*To be a magician, you have to notice that magic is
everywhere.*

Henry looked up at the giant oak trees
surrounding him and watched as their red
and yellow leaves floated down from the sky.

Henry reached into the hat and felt something
furry. It was soft and seemed to be breathing.
He could feel its heartbeat on his fingertips.
Even the squirrels looked up now.

Right as Henry was about to pull out what surely
was a beautiful, gleaming white rabbit, he paused.
"We all know there is a rabbit inside this hat.
I don't need to show it to you. I know it's there.
So, for the trick, I'm going to make it disappear."

Henry turned the hat upside down and nothing came out. He showed the empty hat to his audience. And this time, he heard applause.

It was coming from the kitchen window.
"Bravo, Henry! That was marvelous."

Henry saw his mother smile in a way she hadn't in some time.

"Something from nothing, Mama!" Henry shouted. "It's just like Grandpa said. Isn't it beautiful?"

"Yes, Henry, it is beautiful," his mother said.

Henry carefully put all of his
magical things back into his brown
leather suitcase and snapped it shut.

And then he
heard two truly
magic words:

"Henry. Pancakes."

For Udo, who taught me all
about magic.—J.R.

For my extraordinary parents, Sally and Tom.—D.H.

G. P. Putnam's Sons
an imprint of Penguin Random House LLC
375 Hudson Street
New York, NY 10014

Library of Congress Cataloging-in-Publication Data is available upon request.
Manufactured in China by RR Donnelley Asia Printing Solutions Ltd.
ISBN 9780399257445
1 3 5 7 9 10 8 6 4 2

Design by Michelle Gengaro-Kokmen.
Text set in 16-point Stempel Schneidler Std Medium.
The art in this book was made with watercolor, graphite, colored pencil, and Photoshop.